Teddy's Rhyme & Reason

The Poetic Mewsings of an F.O.T.
(Fabulous Orange Tabby)

Written by Bette-Jean Coderre

Illustrated by Karen S. Marshall

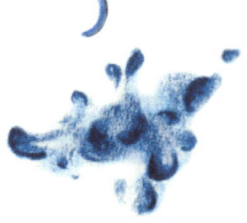

Bette-Jean Coderre is also author of
"Teddy's Tail
The Wit and Wisdom of an F.O.T.
(Fat Orange Tabby)"

In loving memory of MeeMee's

parents, grandparents, brothers, and sister

who exemplified the wisdom of the elders:

Life is a circle.

Walk gently upon the earth in harmony and in balance.

Remember always:

All things are connected.

DEDICATION

This book is dedicated to a man who touches us not only through his music but also through his gentleness and his compassion for people.

His commitment to those who have served our country in times of war and in times of peace is encouraging and moving. His kindness and concern for elders and those less fortunate are traits we can truly emulate.

For touching the hearts of so many people,

I dedicate "TEDDY'S RHYME & REASON" to TONY ORLANDO

for whom there will always be tied "a yellow ribbon around the old oak tree."

© Photograph by Mark Brett

Tony Orlando with Olive Coderre Picozzi

" You are the key to happiness ❗ "

ACKNOWLEDGMENTS

"No one who achieves success does so without acknowledging the help of others."

To all those who helped make *Teddy's Rhyme & Reason* a wonderful reality,

I extend my sincere thanks and appreciation:

Faith Damon Davison for her expertise in editing this book, (Rest in peace, Faithful Friend.)

Veterans for their service and dedication to our country,

Helping Paws for being a veteran's loyal and best friend,

Mensa Cats & Canine Academy Alumni for gracing this book with their beautiful presence,

My Mother, my Father, Bill, Ron, and Beryl who welcomed me into this world

and who inspired me by their love for Mother Earth, justice, and peace,

Karen S. Marshall "fur meow-velously cat-turing my charismatic and purr-found purr-sonality."

The Sisters of St. Joseph with whom I memorized and recited many Maxims of Perfection,

Readers for whom writing this book was a privilege and a pleasure.

Thank you one and all.

Bette-Jean Coderre, SSJA

Teddy's Acknowledgment-osophy:

"If the only prayer you ever say in your entire life is thank you, it will be enough."

POINTS to PONDER

PROLOGUE : ENLIGHTENMENT

It looked easy. But it WASN'T !

A cat writing poetry?

That, Dear Readers, is the reason I matriculated in Mensa Cats Academy. *

Believe you me, it was not all fun and games. I soon learned that everything was not always just BLACK AND WHITE.

Being an only kitty did not prepare me for the challenges of kitty-garten. I wanted to be home schooled, but MeeMee decided I should learn to be with other kitties.

Never in my life did I see so many other kitties. They came in all shapes, sizes, and colors.

MeeMee had a morning ritual. Everyday she would pick me up,

cuddle me, scratch me gently under my chin and say,

"Tedsiekins, I love you to bits.

YOU are UNIQUE in all the world."

Up to this point, I thought this meant I was the only orange kitty in the world.

That, I wasn't. Mensa Cats & Canine Academy was inundated with orange cats.

The few times I did not go home by the paw-mobile transportation, I feared MeeMee would

pick up the wrong orange kitty.

Overcome my fears? Yessiree!
Graduate? Most certainly did!

I am now <u>the</u> Cat-Poet Laureate.
So-o-o-o-o....

Sit down, relax, this book purr-ruse,
and you will surely be amewsed.

* After the spring break, intelligent canines were allowed to enroll.

The school's name was changed to Mensa Cats & Canine Academy.

After all, "Variety is the spice of life."

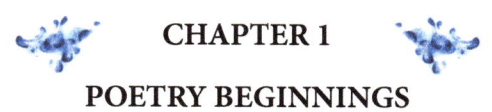
At Mensa Cats and Canine Academy,

I learned to create and write cat-poetry.

I loved making rhymes-

Did it all the time-

At Mensa Cats and Canine Academy.

Teddy's Kitty-garten Life-osophy:

"Always remember that you are absolutely unique,

just like everybody else."

4

Purr & Paws Trans-fur Service

Miss Daisy's Kitty-Garden

WELCOME KITTEN GARDENERS

Hip Hop Garden Maintainance Co.

6

To make a New Year's resolution,

Select the Teddy sage-solution.

It's fun. It gives glee.

It's truly stress-free!

I am done with my elocution.

Teddy's
evolution
of the
dissolution
of the
New Year
resolution

Teddy's Resolution-osophy:

Short is sweet.

a. One.

b. None.

c. Done !

CHAPTER 3

VERACITY

Said my Valentine Cleokatra,

"Teddy, you have POUNDS that are extra.

Deeply disturbing as this sounds,

You truly need to lose those pounds."

That candid cute cat, Cleokatra!

Teddy's Pun-osophy:

RIGHT she was,

so I LEFT.

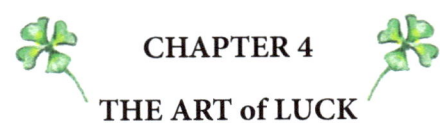

CHAPTER 4
THE ART of LUCK

Here's a truth I advocate,

(Look below, I demonstrate.)

Luck can come so easily,

(I paste my own, gleefully.)

Now make your own. Fabricate.

Teddy's Art-of-Luck-osophy:

Paste. Do not iron.

Never press your luck.

This is such an eggs-citing time of the year!

April Showers and taxes always appear.

I hold it dear that kindness rules

When playing pranks for April Fools.

Hippety! Hoppety! Earth Day! Spring is here.

Teddy's Eggs-osophy:

"Never put all your eggs in one basket."

CHAPTER 6

A-MAYING

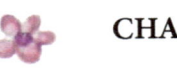

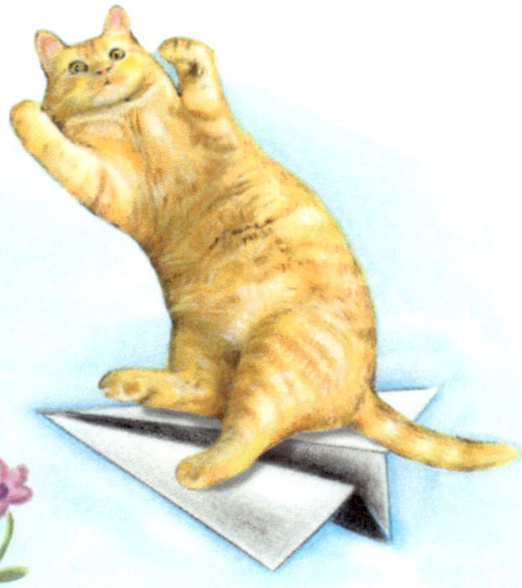

Tis the merry month of a-Maying,
May-day baskets and May-pole swaying,
  Smelling flowers, feeling the breeze,
  Thanking mothers, climbing some trees,
Swinging, jumping, and aviating.

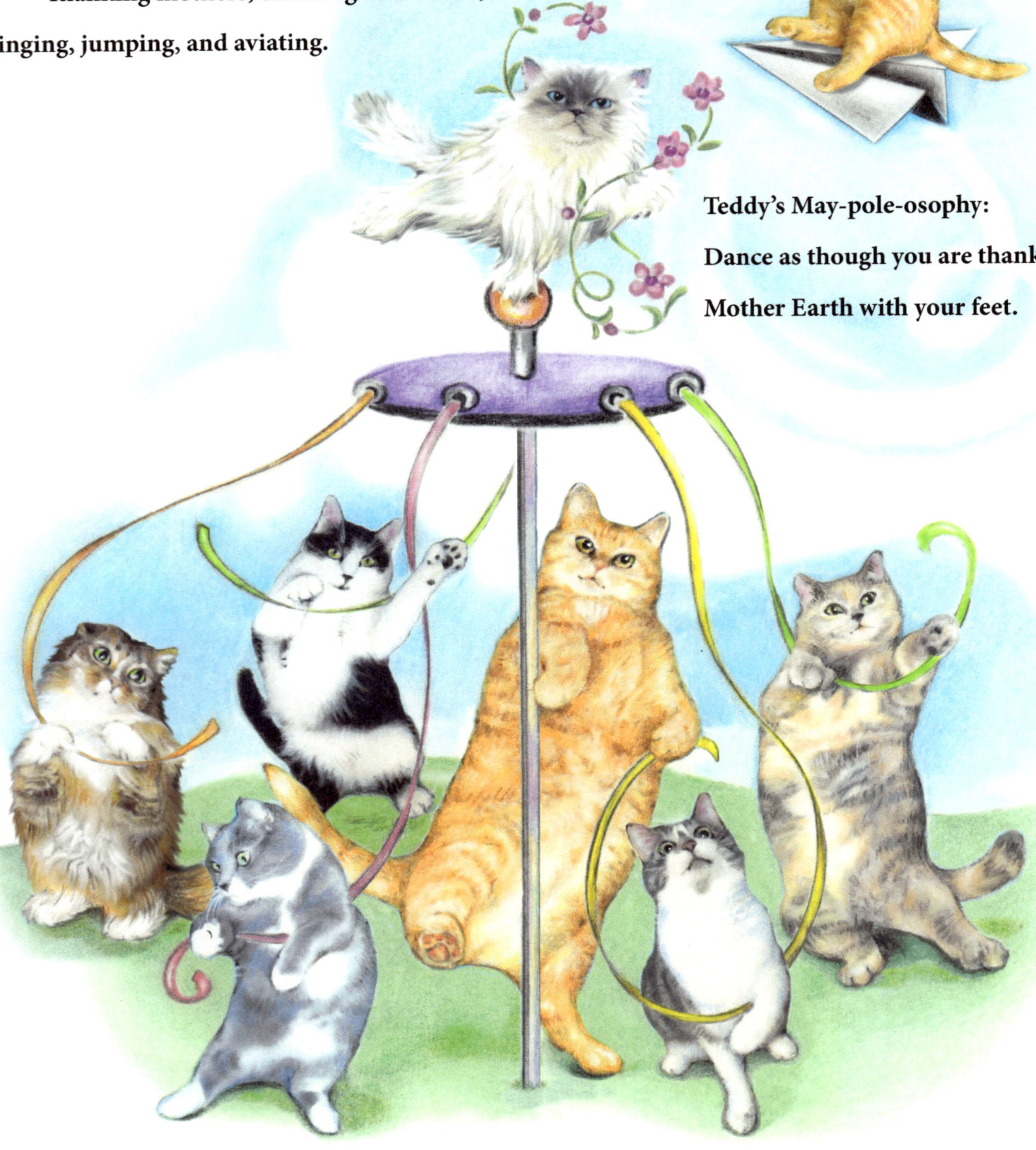

Teddy's May-pole-osophy:
Dance as though you are thanking
Mother Earth with your feet.

CHAPTER 7

LIGHTHEARTEDNESS

Honoring fathers, presenting mugs,

Happiness, picnics, bestowing hugs,

Yo-yo tricks and flying kites,

Honey bees, mosquito bites, 😞

Butterflies, fireflies, and lady bugs.

Teddy's Fun-osophy:

All work and no play is never part of my day.

Hurrah! Hurray! Independence Day!

Fireworks, parades, our flag we display!

Signing my name, tis legendary,

Valorous deed, tis exemplary.

Heroic act! Independence Day!

Teddy's Write Right-osophy:

"Actions speak louder than words."

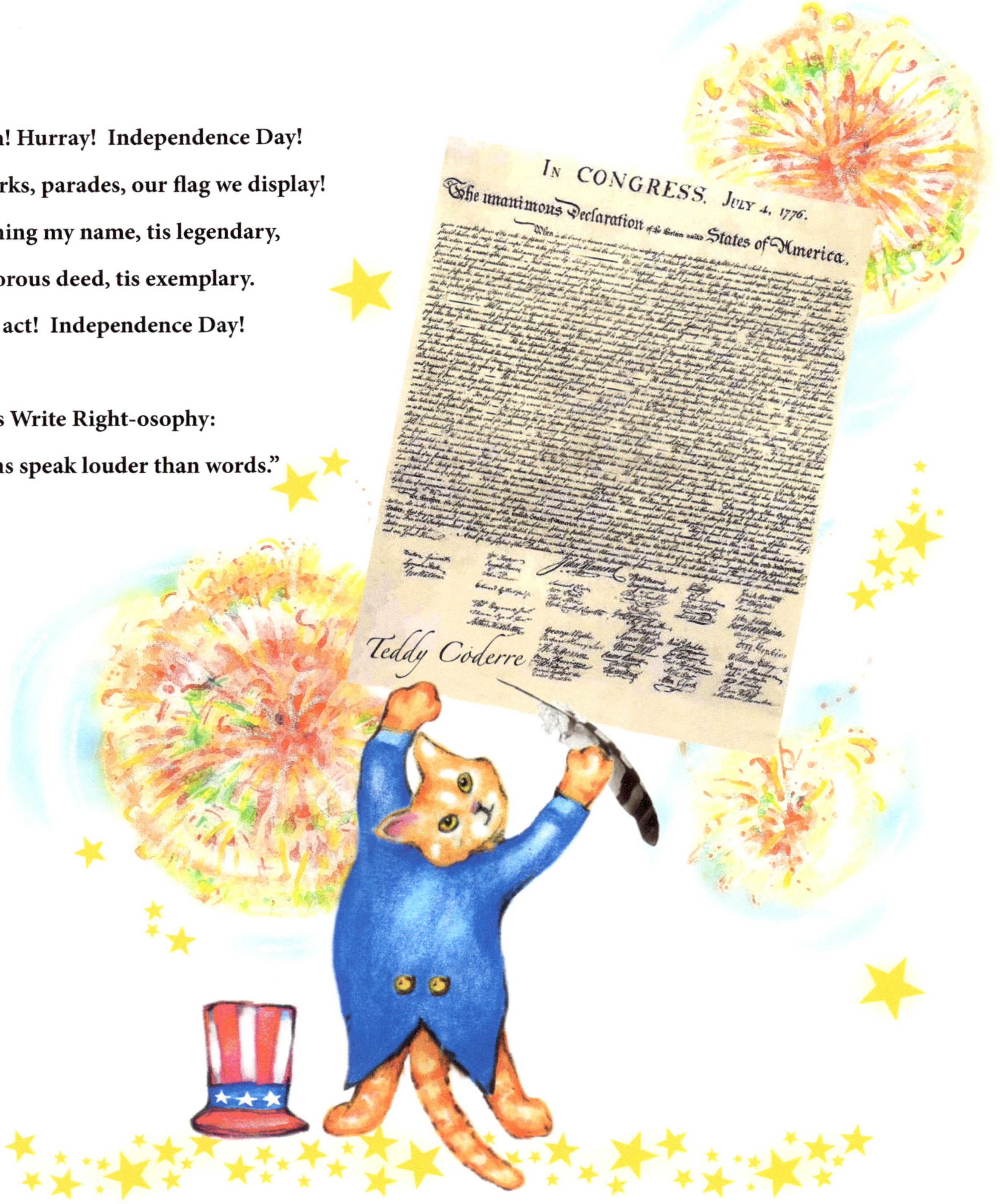

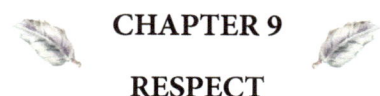

Mother Earth, the gathering of nations,

Honoring our ancestors with elation,

Pow Wow drumming, socializing,

Dancing, singing, storytelling.

Circle of Life! One-drous jubilation!

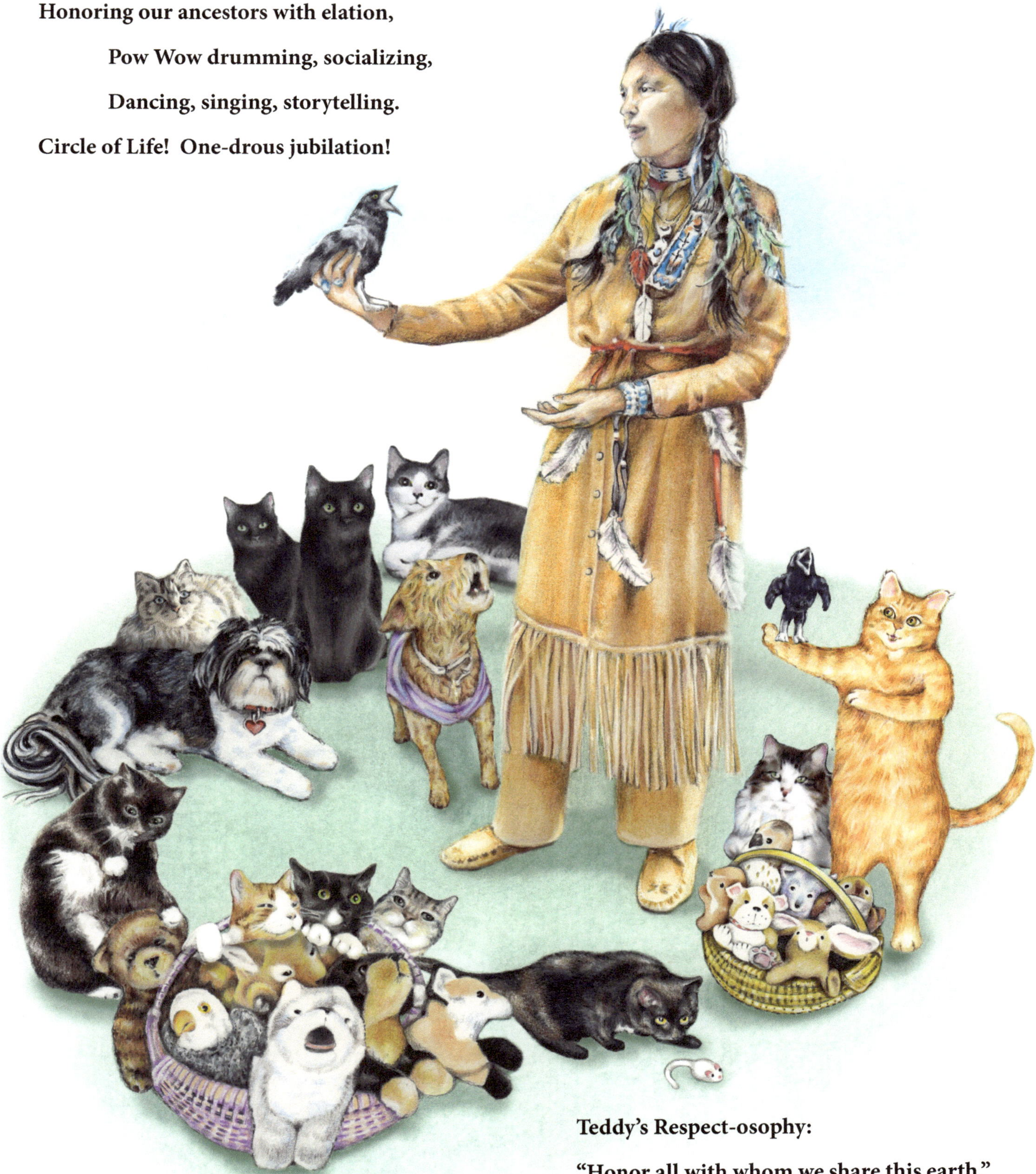

Teddy's Respect-osophy:

"Honor all with whom we share this earth."

CHAPTER 10
NO CHARGE

Teddy and Bilbo Gizmo

Composed a no-charge demo.

For your life to get better,

Embrace words of four letters:

Love, care, hope, help, heal, live, and grow.

Teddy's Value-osophy:

We're not kitting. These words are purr-fect.

They positively *demo-strate*:

"THE COST OF REAL LOVE IS - NO CHARGE."

CHAPTER 11

FALL FAVORITES

Pumpkin carving, apple picking,

Football playing, hiking, camping,

Having fun, climbing trees,

Colorful, falling leaves,

Trick or treating, lots of spooking.

Teddy's Boo-osophy:

"Spook only when spoken to."

WILLIAM MARTIN
US COAST GUARD
CHIEF PETTY OFFICER

RONALD G. CODERRE
"WILD CROW"
US NAVY

WALTER CLARK
US ARMY
WAIST GUNNER/NAVIGATOR

CHARLES ADAMS
US NAVY

Eleventh hour, eleventh day,

Eleventh month, reflect and pray.

Near or far, peace or war,

Much hope they did restore.

Our heads we bow this solemn day.

ALLISON E. HATCHER
US ARMY - FLIGHT MEDIC
COMBAT AVIATION BRIGADE

LCDR JASON S. WARREN
US COAST GUARD

JAMES R. MARSHALL
US AIR FORCE

SEAN ALMONINA D'ANGELO
US NAVY
AIRMAN RECRUIT

YOUR GOOD DEEDS
ARE NEVER FORGOTTEN.

WILLIAM C. CODERRE, JR.
"RUNNING WOLF"
US NAVY

BERT F. KAISER
US MARINE CORPS
MASTER SERGEANT

Teddy's Rainbow-osophy:

"When I cry,

I'll remember to stand in the sun,

so that my tears will become

tiny rainbows."

"All gave some, some gave all."

CMS CLAUDIA JONES
OHIO NATIONAL GUARD
180TH FW

HUBERT LAMPRECHT
US ARMY

W. CLIFTON CODERRE, SR.
US ARMY

JOHN MORGAN
US MARINE CORPS

HELPING PAWS - UNSUNG HEROES

CHARLES C. HARRIS, JR.
"THUNDER CLOUD"
US ARMY

SGT IAN KENNEDY
US ARMY

GEORGE KANE
US ARMY

Bucky, Xena, plus many more,

Undying love they all outpour.

Trustworthy and keen,

Faithful and serene,

Honorable! Four-evermore!

Teddy's Four Paws-osophy:

"The soul that walks in love

neither rests nor grows tired."

19

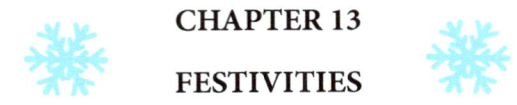

CHAPTER 13
FESTIVITIES

Festivity shopping, crowds galore,

Decorating, laughing, and so much more,

Giving, receiving,

Joy in believing,

Peace on earth - now and forevermore!

Teddy's Present-osophy:

"Be all wrapped up in each other."

CHAPTER 14

TIGER

Once there was a cat named Tiger,

Meemee's friend and first-rate helper.

The liver dinner she did hate,

Her buddy Tiger came and ate.

That terrific cat named Tiger !

Teddy's Friendship-osophies:

"A good friend is a tower of strength:

To find one is to find a treasure."

and

"Make new friends but keep the old.

One is silver and the other is gold."

Birds teach us TREE-mendous, tip top things:

They help each other. They trust their wings.

Let not life pass you by;

Spread your wings.   Fly! Fly! Fly!

Build a nest. Cheer-up. Ev'ry one sings.

Teddy's Eagle-eyed-osophy:

"Become like a bird, expand your wings,

fly as high as you can,

and learn new things."

CHAPTER 16

LIFE'S LESSON: PURRFECTION

At the M-C-C-A facility,

I learned profound purrfect-ability:

Playing and learning,

Sharing and purring,

PURRRRR-fect, quick-witted affability.

Teddy's Purrfect-osophy:

Nobody's perfect.

("I'm nobody. Who are you?")

EPILOGUE: INSIGHT

The happiest moment in my life was my kitty-garten graduation. With all the college graduations that I have celebrated, Dear Readers, you are probably pondering, "Why is Teddy's kitty-garten graduation the most memorable and the most joyful of his graduations?"

On that day when we got home, MeeMee picked me up, hugged me tightly, and said, "Tedsiekins, I know the first day of kitty-garten you were surprised and disappointed to learn that there is a myriad of orange kitties in the world. You were often afraid that I would pick up the wrong orange kitty when you did not go home by the paw-mobile transportation. Tedsiekins, that would NEVER have happened. To me YOU are the ONLY orange kitty in the world. Just as *The Little Prince* had his special rose, I have my special orange kitty.

It is YOU, not the myriad of orange kitties, whom I am raising from kittyhood to cathood;

It is YOU with whom I play fetch and other games;

It is YOU about whom I fret and worry when you are sick;

It is YOU with whom I take walks outside on beautiful days;

It is YOU with whom I laugh and cry;

AND...

It is YOU of whom I am so very proud.

My darling Tedsiekins, to me,

YOU are UNIQUE in all the world,

for YOU are MY orange tabby

forever, and ever, and ever.

Know that

"I will love you forever.

I will like you for always,

and as long as I'm living,"

MY Fabulous Orange Tabby

YOU will be.

Teddy's Insight-osophy:

I <u>am</u> UNIQUE in all the world,

just like everybody else,

but also slightly different.

25

Karen S. Marshall is an illustrator, graphic designer, textile designer, and is a fan of everything Feline!   All of the illustrations presented in *Teddy's Rhyme & Reason* are colored pencil drawings.
Karen lives with her husband Dan in Norwich, Connecticut, where she draws, paints, and is happily purring along with her own kitty, Willow Molly Marshall. When Karen is not drawing, painting, or visiting her many kitty friends, she enjoys practicing yoga, Reiki, and photography.

Bette-Jean Coderre was born in Rhode Island where she grew up to appreciate the smallest of blessings. For over two decades, Bette-Jean was a junior high school teacher in the commonwealth where the first Post Office of the United States was established. (Perhaps, this is why she still mails letters and cards.) Bette-Jean enjoys telling Native American Legends and currently lives in the state where the first phone "book" was made. It is Bette-Jean's heartfelt wish that *Teddy's Rhyme and Reason* uplifts the readers through its "kitting" and osophies.

Teddy's Earnest Earth-osophy Reflection:

"Just as a Turtle is connected to its shell, <u>we</u> are connected to the Earth.
What we do to the earth, we do to ourselves."*
So-o-o-o, Dear Readers, "Love the earth as we have loved it. Care for it as we have cared for it.
<u>And</u> with all your heart, with all your mind, preserve it for the Children."**

*Native American Turtle Story
**Inspired by Chief Seattle

OUR TALENTED CAST OF FURRY CHARACTERS

SCHOOL YARD   pg. 6-7

Top Deck Bus Riders:

Mousie Schultz; Rooster Kuhl; Happy Jack Leonard; Wendell Beisel; Mona Lamprecht; Izzy Wheeler

Kitty Cozy Riders:

Cookie Siekierski; Annie Luering; Moomoo Nyman; Wolf Wolfe; Stanley Springer

Pinwheel Kitty: Leo Paolillo;
Hood Ornament: Cash Harris;
Traffic Light Toppers: Kali Shannon; Cersei Shannon

Bus Riders:
Goldie Thomas; Riley St Aubin; Sammy Knight; Vonda Stanbery; Shelby Goldblatt; Jake Croy

Bus Driver: Ruby Kozak
Laughing Cat: Jack Luering
Happy Running Dog: Peanut Marshall
Backpack and Wagon Pulling Dog: Sammy Woodis
Red Backpack kitty: Nala Thomas
Wagon Riders: Mela Schultz; Izzy Schultz
Red Ball Dog: Stella Lapointe
Tug-of-War Dogs: Kayla Harreys; Boomer Harreys;   Backpack Tug-of-War Puppy: Zoe Accardo

KITTY GARDEN   pg. 6

Top Arch Kittens: Bauer Bond Whiting; Holly Pawlik; Coconut Reyburn;
Carmela Clifford; Henry Sutherland
Arch Bar Kittens: Sebastian Kollar; Esther Clifford
Flower Kittens:
Red Hibiscus: Gracie Brockett; Vergillia DiMartino; Buttercup: Ozzy Doucette
Black-Eyed Susan: Clinker Smythe Gasiorek
Archway Entrance Kittens:
Duncan Barrie; Nicholas Pawlik; Mango Siekierski; Rusty Paolillo
Kitty Garden Teacher, Miss Daisy: Daisy Shaad
Welcome Sign Kittens: Kiwi Siekierski; Pumpkin Buonano
Hip Hop Maintainance Bunnies: Ginger DeSimone; Squirrel Accardo

RESOLUTIONS   pg. 8

New Year's Dog: Simon Cristello

THE ART of LUCK   pg. 10

Leprechaun: Rufus Pereira

EGGS-CITED   pg. 11

Raining Cats & Dogs:
Aby Marshall; Whittaker Clifford; Lexy Bowen; Katie Goldblatt (tax kitty); Ira Pawlik
Umbrella Puppy; Arya Nyman
Basket Dogs: Pixie Baker; P.J. Tousignant; Jessie Pitkow
Chickens: Thelma & Louise Maikshilo

A-MAYING   pg. 12

Maypole Topper: Hunny Cafarelli Gletherow; Paper Airplane Pilot: J.J. Griffin
Maypole Dancers: Teddy Coderre; Ella Santoro; Beatrice Bally; Mia Maikshilo; Joey Bond Whiting;
Maggie Maikshilo

LIGHTHEARTEDNESS   pg. 13

Hali Pratt; Bassie Pratt; Watson Schaffhauser; Mackerel Pratt (Paw Paw); Mycroft Schaffhauser

RESPECT   pg. 15

Clockwise: Teddy Coderre; Donald Damon; Kitty Harris; Lucky Coderre; Thackeray Binx;
Bartelby Binx; Cecil Davison; Saki LaFleur; Roux Petruzelli; Ollie & Katie Murtha;
Smokey Schoen; Daisy Baker

NO CHARGE   pg. 16

Teddy Coderre and his best friend Gizmo Marshall

FALL FAVORITES   pg. 17

Tree Juggler: Rosie Muccelli; Football Catcher: Gretchen Bally; Full Moon Kitty: Frank Pawlik
Apple Picker: Teddy Coderre; Pumpkin Puppy: Marley Moran
Bone Treat Dogs: Betsy & Wedge Hawkins-Bourne
Wookie: Fred deBlok
Kitties: Poki Klammer Hatcher; Maxine Percy Tarvin; Bumpurr Marshall; Macie Pearl Martin

HELPING PAWS UNSUNG HEROES   pg. 19

Service dogs: Xena Kennedy; Bucky Kane

FESTIVITIES   pg. 20

Gift Wrapped Cats: Teddy Coderre; Cleokatra Marshall

A BIRD'S EYE VIEW   pg. 22

Air Glider Operater: Teddy Coderre
Air Glider Rider: Penelope Brockett
Bird Watching Dogs: Scooby Kitco; Marley Kitco

CHARITY PETS   pg. 33

FOSTER PARROTS and the NEW ENGLAND EXOTIC WILDLIFE SANCTUARY
www.fosterparrots.com
Birds: Scarlet Macaw: Mary   Great Green Macaws: Woodstock & Maya
                  Indian Ring-Necked Parakeet: Tulip
Bunnies: Brownie & Ginger   Hedgehog: Mitchell

WOLF PARK   www.wolfpark.org
Wolf :   Chetan

NEW ENGLAND ALL BREED RESCUE   newenglandallbreedrescue@yahoo.com
Dogs: Bubba & Jiggy

COMPASSION for CATS of New London County, Inc.   carrienylen@comcast.net
Kitties: Huey & Dewey

" QUOTES "

"

Acknowledgments: Anonymous; Meister Eckhart

Prologue: Idiom

Chapter 1:   Margaret Mead

Chapter 2:   Teddy-Idiom

Chapter 3:   Pun

Chapter 4:   Idiom

Chapter 5:   Idiom

Chapter 6:   Teddy-Idiom

Chapter 7:   Teddy-Idiom

Chapter 8:   Idiom

Chapter 9:   Native American Elder

Chapter 10:   Harlan Howard's song, "No Charge"

Chapter 11:   Anonymous

Chapter 12:   a. Author Unknown

                b. Attributed to the Korean War veteran &

                purple heart recipient Howard William Osterkamp

                c. Maxim 18 from St. John of the Cross

Chapter 13:   Burton Hill quote

Chapter 14:   Proverb, Traditional Girl Scout Song

Chapter 15:   Anonymous

Chapter 16:   Emily Dickinson

Epilogue: *The Little Prince* by Antoine De Saint Exupèry

                I'll Love You Forever by Robert Munch

Proceeds: Jane Goodall

"

In loving memory of Teddy and Tiger,

all the proceeds from this book will be donated equally to the following charities:

SHRINERS HOSPITALS for CHILDREN

HOPE for PAWS - Animal Rescue

BEST FRIENDS ANIMAL SOCIETY

DEFENDERS OF WILDLIFE

Teddy's cat-tivating altruistic-osophy quote:

"Only if we understand can we care.

Only if we care will we help.

Only if we help shall they be saved."

33

"We will be known forever by the tracks we leave."

Dakota Proverb